First published in the United States of America
in 2020 by Chronicle Books LLC.

Originally published in Japan in 2018 under the title
Soreshika Nai Wake Naidesho by HAKUSENSHA.
English translation rights arranged with HAKUSENSHA, INC.
through Japan Foreign-Rights Centre.

Library of Congress Cataloging-in-Publication Data available.

ISBN 978-1-4521-8322-0

Manufactured in China.

MIX
Paper from
responsible sources
FSC™ C008047

10 9 8 7 6 5 4 3 2 1

Chronicle Books LLC
680 Second Street
San Francisco, California 94107

Chronicle Books—we see things differently.
Become part of our community at www.chroniclekids.com.

THERE MUST BE MORE THAN THAT!

Shinsuke Yoshitake

chronicle books · san francisco

Oh, no!
It's raining.

Dad said it would be
sunny today, but . . .
you can't always trust
grown-ups.

Hi, Brother.

Hey, Sis.
Do you wanna know something?

Our future is
doomed.

Huh?

What does
"future" mean?

"Future" is what
happens later,
like tomorrow or
next year or ten
years from now.

Terrible things are
going to happen
in the future.

That's what a
grown-up told
my friend.

We're going to run out of food because there are too many people.

There will be plagues and wars

and alien invasions. The earth will be destroyed.

By the time we grow up, things are going to be terrible.

No way! Really?!

Grandma . . .
our future is doomed!

Oh, my! Why do
you say that?

DON'T WORRY!

No one really knows what will happen in the future!

Sure, there will be bad things, but there will be lots and lots of good things, too.

Grown-ups act like they can predict the future . . . but they're not always right.

Dad said that it was going to be sunny today, but he was wrong.

See! That's what I mean.

 Grown-ups often tell you to choose one of two things.

But if neither of them seems right . . .

It's okay to find something new on your own!

There are so many possible futures!

You're right. There must be more than just two or three.

Exactly. There must be more than that!

A future with hot dogs every day.

A future where it's okay to spend the day in pajamas.

A future where every Saturday is Christmas.

A future where robots take us everywhere.

A future where someone always catches the strawberry you drop.

A future where someone does your homework for you.

Okay! What are some other possible futures?

Do I have to throw away my shoes when they get too small?

No! I can use them as planters instead!

Will I be pushing carrots to the side of my plate for the rest of my life?

No way! I can ban them when I grow up!

I'm a slow runner, but does that mean I'll never come in first place?

No! I might be "first place" in a funny-face contest!

Will I have to put up with that bully forever?

Nope! He might be abducted by aliens tomorrow!

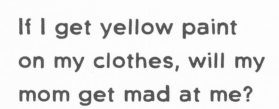
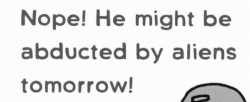

Or, maybe I'll fall in love and I won't even care that I was bullied!

If I get yellow paint on my clothes, will my mom get mad at me?

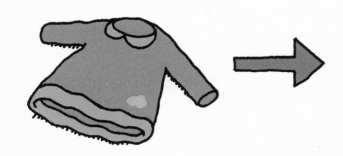

Maybe not if I paint everything else yellow, too!

There are always alternatives, and it's fun to think about what they might be.

Sometimes people ask, "Do you LOVE it or HATE it?" Or, "Is it GOOD or BAD?" Or, "Is that person your FRIEND or your ENEMY?"

But there must be more than just those options!

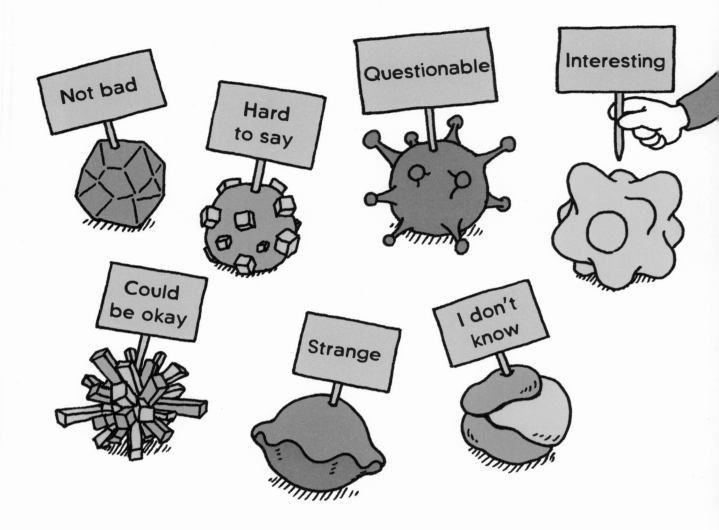

Instead of "love" or "hate," maybe I prefer "lovate!"

I lovate you, Daddy!

Grandma! When I grow up, I'm going to get a job thinking up different futures!

What a great idea!

But . . . I'll probably be gone by then.

No way!

That isn't the only option, Grandma!

Tomorrow, you might feel so great, you could take a trip around the world!

Or, maybe tomorrow you'll wake up as a teddy bear!

Who knows? You could end up living for 300 years!

Hahaha, you're right!
There must be more for me than that!

The future's so
cool, isn't it?

It sure is!

Mom!

Not *just* boiled or fried!

There are more ways to make an egg than that!

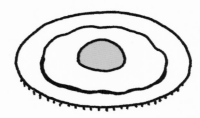

Fried egg

Boiled egg

Omelet

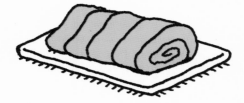

Rolled egg

Scrambled egg

Rolled egg

Rubber band egg

Patted egg

Candy egg

Squeezed egg

Bath egg

Shoe egg

Sticker egg

Painted egg

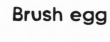

Belly button egg

Mirror egg

Brush egg

Balloon egg

Leaf egg

Cat egg

Book egg

Watch egg

Hmmm . . .

Staring egg

Tied egg

Crown egg

Racing egg

Egg on egg

Towering egg

See?

The future
is full of
possibilities!

Okay, I get it.
I'll make whatever you want.
How would you like your egg?

Hmmm.
I can't decide . . .